BEWARE!

by Diana G. Gallagher

illustrated by Brann Garvey

Claudia Cristina Cortez is published by Stone Arch Books
151 Good Counsel Drive, P.O. Box 669
Mankato, Minnesota 56002
www.stonearchbooks.com

Library of Congress Cataloging-in-Publication Data
Gallagher, Diana G.
  Beware! / by Diana G. Gallagher ; illustrated by Brann Garvey.
    p. cm. — (Claudia Cristina Cortez)
  ISBN 978-1-4342-1575-8
  [1. Bullies—Fiction. 2. Science projects—Fiction. 3. Middle schools—Fiction.
4. Schools—Fiction. 5. Hispanic Americans—Fiction.] I. Garvey, Brann, ill.
II. Title.
  PZ7.G13543Bg 2010
  [Fic]—dc22
                                                2009002546

Summary:
Jenny Pinski is the biggest bully at Pine Tree Middle School. Claudia is paired
up with her for a science project. Some of Jenny's ideas are awful, but Claudia
is afraid to disagree with Jenny. Is her project doomed, or will Claudia find out
there's more to this bully than bullying?

Creative Director: Heather Kindseth
Graphic Designer: Carla Zetina-Yglesias

Photo Credits
Delaney Photography, cover

Printed in the United States of America

Table of Contents

Cast of

ME

CLAUDIA

That's me. I'm thirteen, and I'm in the seventh grade at Pine Tree Middle School. I live with my mom, my dad, and my brother, Jimmy. I have one cat, Ping-Ping. I like music, baseball, and hanging out with my friends.

MONICA is my very best friend. We met when we were really little, and we've been best friends ever since. I don't know what I'd do without her! Monica loves horses. In fact, when she grows up, she wants to be an Olympic rider!

MONICA

BECCA

BECCA is one of my closest friends. She lives next door to Monica. Becca is really, really smart. She gets good grades. She's also really good at art.

ADAM and I met when we were in third grade. Now that we're teenagers, we don't spend as much time together as we did when we were kids, but he's always there for me when I need him. (Plus, he's the only person who wants to talk about baseball with me!)

ADAM

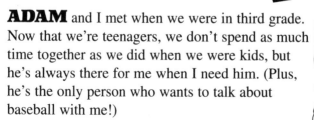

Characters

TOMMY's our class clown. Sometimes he's really funny, but sometimes he is just annoying. Becca has a crush on him . . . but I'd never tell.

I think **PETER** is probably the smartest person I've ever met. Seriously. He's even smarter than our teachers! He's also one of my friends. Which is lucky, because sometimes he helps me with homework.

Every school has a bully, and **JENNY** is ours. She's the tallest person in our class, and the meanest, too. She always threatens to stomp people. No one's ever seen her stomp anyone, but that doesn't mean it hasn't happened!

ANNA is the most popular girl at our school. Everyone wants to be friends with her. I think that's weird, because Anna can be really, really mean. I mostly try to stay away from her.

Cast of

CARLY is Anna's best friend. She always tries to act exactly like Anna does. She even wears the exact same clothes. She's never really been mean to me, but she's never been nice to me either!

NICK is my annoying seven-year-old neighbor. I get stuck babysitting him a lot. He likes to make me miserable. (Okay, he's not that bad ALL of the time . . . just most of the time.)

MR. MONROE is our science teacher. He's also known as the detention king of Pine Tree Middle School! If he catches anyone doing something wrong, they get detention for sure.

Characters

MOM is pretty good at helping me with my problems. I can always count on her.

MOM

DAD

DAD can be kind of a grump, but he's a really good dad. And sometimes he gives me the best advice!

JIMMY is my big brother. I stay out of his way and he stays out of mine.

JIMMY

CHAPTER 1

SCIENCE PROJECT

I was trying to get to my desk, but the classroom aisle was blocked by **a pair of legs**.

Carly Madison was sitting on a desk. Her feet rested on the chair in the next row. She was talking to Anna Dunlap.

Anna Dunlap was Carly's best friend. She also **reigned supreme** over the seventh grade at Pine Tree Middle School.

Q: Why?

A. Anna is popular.

Q. Why is Anna popular?

A. I have no idea.

Anna was bossy, selfish, and stuck up.

But age 13 + popular = teen power.

Most kids wouldn't go against Anna. No way, no how. But my **grandma** always says there are exceptions to every rule.

There were two exceptions to Anna Rules: **me** and Jenny Pinski.

Jenny Pinski was our class bully. She STOMPED kids that make her mad. Or, at least, she said she was going to.

I never stomped anyone. I just didn't care if Anna thought I was a loser-nobody. **I didn't care if Anna liked me.** My friends liked me, and they didn't ignore me.

"Excuse me, Carly," I said.

Carly didn't look at me. She just kept talking to Anna. "Did you see that video game guy on *Teen Trends* last night?" Carly asked.

"**What a dork!**" Anna said. She rolled her eyes. "Who cares if he's the best-ever player of *Wizard Ways*? He wears a tie!"

"My desk is in this row," I said. "Can I get by?"

"They're making a *Wizard Ways* movie," Carly told Anna. *She didn't care if I had to wait.* I gave up and turned to go around.

Anna whispered to Carly, "Claudia is so RUDE."

Actually, Carly and Anna were being rude, but I **never picked fights for stupid reasons.** Sometimes it was wiser to just walk away.

Especially in **Mr. Monroe's** science class.

He held the Pine Tree Middle School record for most detentions given in one day: **22**. I didn't want to risk starting a fight and landing in detention.

I doubled back and walked up the next aisle to my desk next to **Becca**, one of my best friends.

"Uh-oh," Becca muttered. "This will be interesting."

"What?" I asked. I stopped and looked back.

Jenny walked up the blocked aisle.

Carly didn't see Jenny. Not right away. She just kept talking.

"Mom took me to the mall yesterday," Carly said.

"Did you get any new clothes?" Anna asked.

"I found a pair of jeans I **just love**,"
Carly said. "But I have to wait for my birthday."

Anna gasped. "That's horrible!"
she said. **I rolled my eyes.**

"I know, but it's only two more weeks," Carly said.
Then she noticed Jenny. "Oh, hey, Jenny," she said
nervously.

"Get out of the way," Jenny said.

Carly gulped. Then she lowered her
feet to let Jenny pass.

"Carly is such a **WIMP**, isn't she?" Becca
whispered to me.

"Well, gosh, Becca," I whispered back. "Anna and
Carly can't get stomped. Their clothes might get dirty.
And it would mess up their hair!"

I was being sarcastic. Anna and Carly were snobs,
but they were not fools. Only fools gave Jenny Pinski a
hard time. Everybody knew that. You had to stay out
of Jenny Pinski's way.

Or else.

I'd known Jenny since kindergarten. She was a bully back then, too.

Things Jenny Stomped On the First Day of Kindergarten

1. Drinking cups

2. Tinker-toys

3. Cookies

No one had ever seen Jenny stomp a person, but that didn't mean it never happened. A stompee would never tell. It would be too embarrassing.

I never talked to Jenny unless I absolutely had to. The strangest little things upset her.

You never knew if something you said was going to make her mad. For instance:

1. "Your shoe's untied."

2. "I'll trade my banana for your apple."

3. "Do we have math homework?"

Like I said, everybody knew you had to stay out of Jenny Pinski's way. Unless you wanted to get stomped.

When class started, Mr. Monroe announced the big science project.

He said that it was going to count for 25% of our semester grade.

He split the class into teams of two.

1. Monica & Becca

2. Adam & Tommy

3. Peter & Sylvia

4. Anna & Carly

5. Claudia & Jenny.

CHAPTER 2

THE PINSKI PROBLEM

Someone had to be Jenny's project partner.

But why did it have to be me?

Only one word described how I felt:

Doomed!

I tore out a piece of notebook paper and wrote a note to Becca.

WHAT AM I GOING TO DO?

I was going to pass the note to Becca, but **Mr. Monroe** has **built-in bad behavior radar.** He saw me fold the piece of paper. Then he raised his eyebrow and stared at me. He glanced at the pad of detention slips sitting on his desk.

I gulped.

Detention was a crime in my family. Jimmy got detention once in fifth grade and he was grounded for a week.

If I got detention, my dad would:

1. Ground me

(Until I left home for college.)

2. Take away TV

(Until Musical Idol was over for the season.)

3. Give me the silent treatment

(Until I begged for forgiveness and promised to never, ever get detention again.)

I used the note as a bookmark.

I had history after science. Becca and Monica were in that class with me.

"You guys have to come over after school," I told them. "Meet me at the tree house. We've got to talk about my **Jenny Pinski problem.**"

* * *

After school, Monica and Becca came over to my house. We climbed up into the tree house for privacy.

"Having Jenny Pinski for a project partner is the **worst luck ever,**" I said.

"What's wrong with **Jenny pinhead**?" a familiar voice asked. I looked over at the treehouse door. My seven-year-old neighbor, Nick, was sitting on the ladder. As usual, **he wasn't invited** — he'd just snuck up to the tree house.

"It's **Pinski**, not **pinhead**," I said. "What are you doing here?"

"Your mom told me to play outside," Nick said.

If Nick's mom was busy, my mom babysat Nick. If my mom was busy, she made me watch him. **I didn't think that was fair**, but at least sometimes she paid me two dollars an hour.

"Go away, Nick," I said. "We're busy."

Nick didn't answer, and he didn't move. I acted like Carly and ignored him. Then I realized that Nick Wright and Jenny Pinski are a lot alike.

She's the biggest bully at Pine Tree Middle School.

He's the biggest brat in my neighborhood.

They both like to get even.

"Maybe working with Jenny won't be so bad," **Becca** said.

I could usually find **a bright side**. No matter how bad my problems seemed. Not this time.

"It'll be horrible," I said. "I want a good grade."

"Everybody wants a good grade," Monica said.

"What if Jenny doesn't?" I asked. "**What if she hates my ideas**? What if she wants to do something with plants?"

Becca gasped. "I hope she doesn't!" she said.

"Yeah," **Monica** agreed. "We're doing a plant project."

"I want to do something nobody's done before," I said. "Like **train a mouse to spin a wheel to power a light bulb**."

"That sounds cool!" Nick exclaimed.

"It's been done," Monica said.

"The **mouse-bulb** got an A+ last year," Becca explained.

"Choosing a project isn't **your biggest problem**," Monica pointed out.

"It isn't?" I asked nervously.

"Nope," Monica said. She shook her head. "Working with Jenny for two weeks is the problem."

Becca nodded. "You're definitely going to say or do something that **makes Jenny mad**," she said. "There's no doubt about it."

They were probably right. I sighed. "Jenny is going to stomp me for sure," I said sadly.

"**Stomp her first**," Nick said. "Then she won't stomp you."

"That won't work with Jenny," Becca said.

"She's too **MEAN**," Monica added.

Nick shrugged. "It worked with Caroline O'Brien," he said.

"Who's Caroline O'Brien?" I asked.

"She's in my class," Nick said. "I used to pull her hair and call her **Turpentine**."

"That's not nice," Monica said.

Nick shrugged. "I don't do it anymore."

"Why not?" I asked.

"Caroline shoved me," Nick explained. "I fell in a PUDDLE, and everybody laughed. It was awful!"

Bravo for Caroline! She had fought back, and Nick had backed down.

But beating Jenny to the punch wouldn't help me. It would just get me in trouble and make Jenny **madder**.

CHAPTER 3

PROJECT PERIL

My **dad** says dreaming is like cleaning out a closet. We **throw away** things we don't need. We tuck away fond memories for safekeeping. And we try to **hide the bad stuff.**

The bad stuff creeps back in our **NIGHTMARES**.

My mom had tropical fish when she was my age. She loved them, but fish don't live very long. She hated finding dead ones floating in the aquarium. So she gave her fish tank to a friend.

Mom's Forgotten Fish Dream

1. Mom finds fish tanks behind walls.

2. They've been there for years.

3. The plants grew into underwater jungles.

4. All the fish are fine.

Fish tank dream = *guilt for giving away fish*

My older brother liked his computer more than anything. He played complicated online games.

Computers crash a lot, so he had backup drives and anti-virus programs. But **Jimmy** still worried about losing his data, even when he was asleep.

Jimmy's Techno Night Terrors

1. A monster virus swallows his computer whole.

2. A clown virus trashes all his files and laughs.

3. A big-tooth virus eats his flash drive.

Bad computer dreams = something could go wrong

I have nightmares about Jenny Pinski. It started in kindergarten. I took a toy out of Jenny's cubby. She wasn't there, but I was sure she had seen me.

My 1st Pinski Nightmare

1. Jenny stomps all my toys and breaks them.

2. I hide under the covers so she doesn't stomp me.

3. She rips off my blanket.

4. I wake up screaming!

In fourth grade, I hit Jenny with a dodge ball when she wasn't looking. She had to leave the game.

My 2nd Pinski Nightmare

1. I'm a dodge ball.

2. Jenny throws me against the wall over and over again.

3. *I wake up screaming.*

I was Jenny's science project partner. Something bad was bound to happen. That night, I dreamed about it.

My 3rd (and probably not my last) Pinski Nightmare

1. Jenny ruins our science project.

2. She pops a huge balloon.

3. A hundred toads fall out on my head.

4. Raining toads = being stomped and slimed!

5. *I wake up screaming!*

My 3rd Pinski Nightmare: *Part 2*

1. Jenny dips our project report in purple paint.

2. She tells Mr. Monroe I did it.

3. A lightning bolt shoots from his finger.

4. A purple F blazes on my forehead.

5. I wake up shouting, "No!"

Jenny Pinski nightmares = 7th grade nervous breakdown!

* * *

I was **totally freaked out** when Jenny came to my house the next day after school. She didn't knock. She banged on the door. Then she barged in when I opened it.

"This better not take too long," Jenny said. "I want to get home."

Five seconds was too long for me!

"It won't," I said. "We just have to pick a project."

"What do you want?" Jenny asked. She flopped on the sofa.

"I want to **get an A**," I said honestly.

"I don't want to be BORED," Jenny said. "Got any ideas?"

I had a few ideas, but I didn't know if Jenny would think they were boring. "We could test batteries to see which brand lasts the longest," I suggested.

"Why bother?" Jenny asked.

"Because batteries go bad at the worst times," I explained nervously. "Like, you know, when the power goes out and you need a flashlight to use the bathroom."

Jenny stared at me.

"And changing flashlight batteries in the dark is hard," I said.

"BORING," Jenny said. She folded her arms. "What else?"

I blurted out the words before I could stop myself. "Well, another idea I had was testing laundry detergents," I said.

Jenny frowned. That was a bad sign.

I rushed to explain. "My mom wants to know which brand really takes out grass stains," I said. "My brother mows lawns, and he **ruins** all of his T-shirts. There's no way to get the shirts clean."

"I don't do laundry," Jenny said. "I want to do our project on something EXCITING."

"We could build a contraption that takes fresh water out of salt water," I said. "We can make it with stuff we find around the house. I saw an article about it in a magazine."

"What's exciting about that?" Jenny asked. "Who on earth cares about making fresh water out of salt water?"

I thought fast. "What if you're stranded on a desert island?" I asked. "It would help. You can't drink salt water, so unless you were able to make fresh water, you'd die!"

"I'll drink **bottled water** if I ever get stranded on a desert island," Jenny said.

"There isn't any bottled water on a desert island," I argued.

"There isn't any **household stuff**, either," Jenny pointed out.

That was true. I gave up. "Do you have a better idea?" I asked.

Jenny's eyes narrowed. **She looked mad.** "I might, you know," she said.

"I know," I said quickly.

Jenny thought for a minute. Then she looked at me.

"Let's make up a PLANET," she suggested.

That sounded kind of weird, but I nodded and said, "Okay."

Anything that would keep Jenny **excited and not bored** was okay with me.

"We can make a model and dioramas to go with our report," Jenny said. "We have to decide what kind of planet it is. Then we can make up plants and animals that might live on it. **Mr. Monroe will love it.** I just know it."

"That's a good idea," I said.

"Glad you think so," Jenny said. "Because that's the project we're doing."

After Jenny left I wondered: Did I **really** like Jenny's idea? Or was I **pretending** so I wouldn't get STOMPED?

I couldn't tell.

CHAPTER 4

TABLE FOR TWO

Jenny and I sat together at lunch on Monday. We had to write a project summary.

"Doing a report about doing a report is STUPID," Jenny complained.

"Mr. Monroe has to **approve** all the projects," I said.

Some past Pine Tree Middle School projects hadn't worked out.

Smart Kids Do Dumb Stuff

Or

How to Make a Good Science Project Go Bad

1. Stink up the science lab

2. Spray yucky stuff everywhere

3. Set animals loose in the gym

My brother, Jimmy, used his **pet snake, Stanley,** for his seventh grade project. One morning, Stanley was gone. Only his shed skin was left in the tank in the science lab.

The janitor finally found the snake **safe and sound** in a huge box of pencils. But nobody used their lockers for a week!

I didn't tell Jenny about Stanley. I didn't want to give her any ideas. She might want to create **The Planet Project Creature that Stomped the Science Teacher.**

"Do you want to take notes?" I asked.

"You do it," Jenny said. "You can write the summary, too."

That was okay with me. I like to write, and I didn't want to argue with Jenny. Besides, I still wanted an A.

I turned to get my notebook. Becca and Monica walked by with their lunch trays.

"Hi! Do you want to sit with us?" I asked. "We've got **plenty of room.**" No one else was sitting at our table.

"Well, uh —" Monica looked at Becca. "We've got to talk about our project summary."

"That's what we're doing!" I exclaimed.

"Tommy and Adam are **waiting** for us," Becca said. "See you later!"

I usually sit with my friends at our regular table. **I didn't like being left out.** But Jenny and I had work to do.

"I think this project will be fun," I said. "It'll be just like making up an **alien planet** for a movie."

"Exactly like that," Jenny said. "I think **Weird World** should have silicon-based life forms."

"What's that?" I asked.

"Animals and plants that are made of rock and crystals," Jenny explained. "We can write the summary like we're **EXPLORERS**. We land in a rocket ship and take a tour!"

I knew Mr. Monroe wouldn't let us do that. He wanted real science. I had to squash Jenny's idea without making her mad.

"**Simple is better,**" I said. "Like your first idea. Instead of rockets, our project should be about the rock science of Weird World. Mr. Monroe will love that."

Jenny frowned. "Does that mean we can't have rock monsters?" she asked.

"Probably not," I said. I quickly added, "But we can have **rock people** and **rock animals**."

"And **pet rocks**!" Jenny said. She laughed.

I had never heard Jenny laugh before. I was so surprised I gagged on my sandwich. When I stopped coughing, I said, "I like pet rocks."

"I didn't think that up," Jenny said. "I found it on the Internet. People used to have them. "

I blinked. "When did people have pet rocks?" I asked.

"Back in the 1970s," Jenny said. "A guy painted eyes on stones, put them in little boxes, and sold them as pets. **He made lots of money.** Then people figured out they could make their own pet rocks, I guess."

"We can too," I said. "We can have a diorama with a **rock family** and a rock pet."

"That works," Jenny said. She held up her hand for a high-five.

When the bell rang, I had enough notes to write a good summary. **It was due the next day.**

Jenny and I left the cafeteria together. Anna and Carly were standing in the doorway.

"Come on, Sylvia!" Anna yelled. "We'll be **LATE**!"

"Just a sec!" Sylvia called back.

Sylvia was the school slow-poke. **She wasn't lazy.** She was just never in a hurry. She carefully took all the garbage off her tray and threw it away.

"I'm not waiting for Sylvia," Jenny said. She stomped toward the door. **"Coming through!"**

Anna and Carly both stepped back so Jenny and I could walk out.

One good thing about being with Jenny: When you were with her, everybody got out of your way in a hurry.

Becca and Monica were talking to Tommy and Adam by the drinking fountain. We always walk to English together. I thought they were waiting for me. Suddenly, they turned away and HURRIED down the hall.

Peter rushed past me. He always smiles and says, "Hi!" Not this time. **He just kept going**, even though I smiled at him.

I wanted to think my friends just hadn't seen me.

But I knew they had.

They had seen me with Jenny.

CHAPTER 5

AVOIDING JENNY

I went to my locker after the last bell. Becca and Monica weren't there yet. We usually met at my locker every day after school. **They were never late.**

Soon, Adam walked up.

"What's going on, Claudia?" Adam asked.

"I'm waiting for Becca and Monica," I said. "Have you seen them?"

"Not since our last class," Adam said.

They were late, and **I was worried**.

"I've got practice. Call me later," Adam said suddenly. **He turned and hurried away.**

Two seconds later, someone tapped my shoulder.

I thought it was Becca or Monica. I looked back, saw Jenny, and G𝔸𝔖ℙ𝔼𝔻.

"What's wrong?" Jenny asked.

"Nothing!" I said. I shook my head. "I wasn't expecting anyone to sneak up behind me. **Not that you're sneaky.** You're not. I was just surprised." I talk too much when I'm nervous. "You can surprise me any time you want."

Jenny stared at me for a second. It seemed like an hour. My knees started shaking.

"Here's my **phone number**," Jenny said. She handed me a folded paper. "Call me when the summary's done. I want to know what it says."

I took the paper. "Can I call if I need **HELP**?" I asked nervously.

"Yeah," Jenny said. "Just don't call during *Zombie Zip Code*. That's my favorite show."

I waited while Jenny walked away. Then Larry Kyle rushed out of a classroom. He saw Jenny and flattened against the wall. He didn't move until she was gone.

I didn't blame Larry for staying out of Jenny's way. Jenny was the **tallest girl** in Pine Tree Middle School. She was taller than most of the boys. Larry was the **shortest kid**, and Jenny towered over him.

Plus she's the **school bully**. That's why I got nervous when Jenny startled me.

But that wasn't fair. Jenny had been my project partner for a few days. She hadn't done anything mean. She only wanted to give me her phone number so we could work on our project.

I felt like a jerk.

My friends were waiting for me outside. Becca waved and smiled when I walked out the door.

"Over here, Claudia!" Monica called out.

"Where were you?" I asked as we walked down the sidewalk. "I waited by my locker."

"I didn't need to go to my locker today," Becca said.

"I didn't either," Monica added.

Fact: Monica, Becca, and I meet at our lockers every day, even if we don't have books to drop off.

Claudia's Lie Detector: Lie.

Conclusion: Something was wrong.

"We don't have English homework," I said. "Mrs. Sanchez didn't give us a reading assignment. You could have put your English book in your locker."

Becca turned red.

"I might read ahead," Monica said.

Fact: Monica reads horse books for fun, not textbook stories.

Claudia's Lie Detector: Could be true, but probably not.

Conclusion: Monica didn't want to explain why she and Becca waited outside.

Monica didn't have to explain. I knew why they snubbed me. It happened three times already.

"Were you afraid I might be with Jenny?" I asked.

Becca stared at her feet.

"What do you mean?" Monica asked.

"You didn't sit with me at lunch," I said. "And I was with Jenny. Then you ran ahead of us to fifth period."

Becca shrugged. She didn't want to answer.

Monica confessed in a **gush of guilt**. "Yes, we ran away," she said. "It was a horrible thing to do, but I get all nervous when I'm around Jenny."

"I've been 𝔸𝔽ℝ𝔸𝕀𝔻 of Jenny since kindergarten," Becca said. "She almost stomped Ronnie Carver. She made him cry."

I remembered that too. "Ronnie deserved it," I said.

"I know," Becca said. She sighed. "He called her **Jenny the Giant** a hundred times a day."

"She was a lot taller than everyone back then, too," I said.

"And she was a lot *meaner* than everyone else, too," Becca added, nodding. "But it worked. Ronnie stopped calling Jenny names."

"He wasn't very nice," I said. "Nobody missed Ronnie when he moved away."

"I tried to be nice to Jenny once in second grade," Monica said. **"That was a mistake."**

"What happened?" Becca asked.

"Jenny couldn't open her milk carton," Monica explained. "She got really mad when I offered to help."

Becca's eyes widened. **"Did she stomp you?"** she asked.

Monica shook her head. "No, she said, 'I'm not helpless!' Then she squashed my chocolate cake with her fist."

Becca winced.

Monica shuddered. "I was sure she was going to punch me. **That was the scariest thing that ever happened to me**," she said.

"Scarier than the Halloween Haunted House at the Community Center when we were little?" I asked.

"Yes," Monica said. "Even when we were little, I knew that the Haunted House was fake. **Jenny Pinski is real.**"

CHAPTER 6

PEER PRESSURE

That night, I called Jenny when I finished the project summary. I read the title first. **"Is Rock Life Possible?"**

"Who cares?" Jenny exclaimed.

"Huh?" I asked. "We care, don't we? I mean, that's why we're doing this project, right?"

"Yeah, but that title is so **boring** that nobody else will care," Jenny said.

She had a point. "Okay, you're right. It's boring. What should we do instead?" I asked.

"We need something with PUNCH," Jenny replied. "Something that will get people interested. Like this. **Weird World: A Planet Where Rocks Rule.**"

"Perfect!" I told her. I crossed out my title and wrote down the new one.

"Mr. Monroe better like it **or I'll be mad**," Jenny said.

I was pretty sure Jenny wouldn't mess with a teacher. But I wasn't positive, and I didn't want to ask. So I read the rest of my summary.

Luckily, **Jenny loved it**! I was safe from being stomped for another day.

* * *

The next day, Mr. Monroe collected our written summaries. Then he asked everyone to give an oral report to the class. Jenny was the first person to raise her hand.

"Claudia and I are **making up a planet** where living rocks exist," Jenny said.

"That sounds interesting," Mr. Monroe said. "Who's next?"

Adam and Tommy's project was called **The Best Bounce**. They were going to test how high different balls bounced on different surfaces. "We'll use all different sizes of balls," Adam explained.

Mr. Monroe said, "Just be careful to not break anything."

Peter and Sylvia planned to study how people, animals, and plants reacted to music and noise.

"What about you, Anna?" Mr. Monroe asked.

"Carly and I want to find out how plants act in different conditions," Anna said.

"That's just like our project," Monica exclaimed.

"We said it first so we have **dibs**," Anna argued.

"*No one has dibs,*" Mr. Monroe said. "I don't want two teams doing the same project. Each team will have to come up with a new idea by tomorrow."

Anna and Carly stopped Becca and Monica in the hall before lunch.

Jenny came up behind me again. I didn't jump this time. Not even when she whispered in my ear, **"What's going on?"**

"I'm not sure," I whispered back.

"We need to talk, Monica," Anna said.

"Talk about what?" Monica asked.

Anna smiled.

Alert! Anna only smiles when she wants something. Watch out!

"Do you have another project idea?" Anna asked.

"Maybe," Monica said, "but I'm not telling what it is." I could tell **she didn't trust Anna**.

"I don't care what it is," Anna said.

"Good," Becca said. "Because it's none of your business." **She didn't trust Anna either.**

"Since you have a new idea, I want to keep the plant project," Anna said.

"Mr. Monroe told 𝓑𝓞𝓣𝓗 teams to think up something new," Monica said.

"Yeah, because he doesn't want two teams doing the same project," Anna said. "So if Carly and I do the plant project, we won't be doing the same thing. You'll be doing the new project you came up with. It's totally fair. Mr. Monroe just doesn't want you to do the plant project because ours will be better and you'll feel bad."

"You've got something else, Monica," Carly said. "It's **mean and unfair** not to let us do the plant project."

Monica frowned. "We're not 𝕄𝔼𝔸ℕ," she said.

"Or **unfair**," Becca added.

Anna shrugged. "Everyone will think you are when I tell them you won't let us have a project you're not using. And I'll tell them you **cheated**, too. I'll tell them you stole the idea from me."

"We didn't cheat," Becca said.

"And you don't even know what our idea is," Monica said.

"No one will believe you," Anna told her. "Trust me."

"Fine, Anna," Becca said. "You can do the plant project."

"Our new idea is a lot better anyway," Monica added.

"Whatever," Anna said. She walked into the cafeteria. Carly followed her.

"Come on, Becca," Monica said. "We've got a new project to talk about."

I could tell Becca and Monica were **embarrassed**. Anna had blackmailed them to get the plant project.

"They should have told Anna to get lost," Jenny said.

I knew it wasn't that easy. Jenny didn't care if everyone thought she was mean. Becca and Monica did.

And Anna wasn't **bluffing**. She was the most popular girl in the seventh grade. If she spread a rumor, everyone would believe it. **Even if it wasn't true.**

CHAPTER 7

THE BEST REVENGE

Jenny came to my house Monday afternoon. We were going to start our Weird World project.

Every project has three steps.

1. Decide what to do.

2. Decide who does it.

3. Do it.

Jenny had already decided what to do.

"I want to make a model of the planet," Jenny said. "I've got it all figured out."

"Okay," I said.

"We need a chart, too," Jenny added.

"Definitely," I agreed. "Mr. Monroe loves charts."

So far our meeting was going **a lot better** than I expected. It didn't last.

"He'll like dioramas even better," Jenny said.

"I LOVE making dioramas!" I exclaimed.

Jenny had already decided who should do what, too. "I'll be the one who makes the model and the chart and the dioramas," Jenny said. "You can write the report."

I paused. Jenny had picked our project idea. Now she was taking over the whole thing. **Numbers 1, 2, and 3!** I knew it wasn't wise to argue with her, but we were a team.

"Okay, I'll write the report," I agreed. "But I also want to work on the dioramas."

Jenny didn't get mad. But she didn't give in, either. "No," she said, shaking her head.

"Why not?" I asked. **"I make good ones."**

"Maybe, but your style is different," Jenny said. "The dioramas should look like a matched set."

That made sense, but **I wasn't happy.** "I really want to work on the dioramas," I told her. "That's the fun part."

"You can print the index cards and labels," Jenny suggested. "So they'll match."

"Okay, but that won't be much fun," I complained.

Jenny frowned.

My heart thumped. Uh-oh!

Then something STRANGE happened.

"You're right," Jenny admitted. "Printing is boring. Do you want to help make rock candy?"

I was stunned.

1. Jenny wasn't mad.

2. She understood my point.

3. She wanted to make me feel better!

"Sure!" I said. "Why are we making rock candy?"

"Rock candy is just a bunch of sugar crystals," Jenny said. "It shows how inorganic stuff can grow."

"Wow!" I said. I was impressed. "So there really could be **rock creatures** on another planet."

"Could be," Jenny said.

Just then, **Nick** ran in. He stood in front of Jenny and stared.

Important Point: Nick only cares about getting what he wants.

Jenny stared back.

Important Point: She doesn't let anyone get the best of her.

The Bully and The Brat

Jenny threatens to stomp.

No one has ever been stomped.

That we know of.

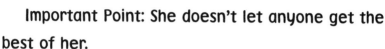

Nick doesn't threaten.

He punches and kicks.

I have scars to prove it.

I watched Nick and Jenny stare each other down. It was like waiting for a firecracker to go off.

The contest could only end one way. With a BANG!

"I like candy," Nick said.

"Get lost," Jenny said.

Nick blinked. Then he spun around and ran away.

Another good thing about being with Jenny: Nick runs away from her.

"He'll be back," I said.

"Not today," Jenny said. She grinned.

"Don't count on it," I said.

The doorbell rang, and I opened the door. Becca and Monica rushed in.

"We've got a BIG problem," Monica said.

"How big?" Jenny asked.

Becca and Monica stopped dead when they saw Jenny Pinski in my living room.

"We didn't know you were busy," Becca said.

"We're done," Jenny said.

"What's the problem, Monica?" I asked.

Monica didn't answer. **She looked really nervous.** She kept looking at Jenny and then at me.

Nick marched back in wearing *a pot on his head*. He banged a lid with a big spoon.

I grabbed the spoon to stop the noise.

"I need that!" Nick yelled. He glared at me.

"What for?" I asked.

"**A duel.** With her!" Nick screamed. He pointed at Jenny.

"No way, kid," Jenny said. "You're too 𝕋𝕆𝕌𝔾ℍ for me."

"Good," Nick said. He sat in my dad's chair. He took the pot off his head. He kept the spoon and lid in his lap.

Monica and Becca exchanged a look. Then they sat down.

"So **what's the matter**?" I asked again.

"We don't have a new project idea," Becca said.

"You told Anna and Carly that you did," I said.

Monica sighed. "I just let Anna think I did," she admitted.

"Why?" I asked. "You have to think up a project and write a new summary. **Anna and Carly don't have to do anything.** Their plant project summary is done."

"You shouldn't let Anna push you around," Jenny said.

"Anna said she'd tell everyone we were *mean and selfish* and that we **cheated** on the project," Becca said.

"So what?" Jenny asked. She shook her head. **"It doesn't matter what other kids think."**

"Yes, it does," Nick said. "Caroline O'Brien calls me a pea-brain, and I'm not."

"Pretend you don't care," Jenny said. "She'll stop."

"She will?" Nick asked.

"I'm pretty sure," Jenny said. "But if she doesn't, all you have to do is THREATEN —"

"To walk away!" I shouted.

I didn't want Jenny to tell Nick to threaten to stomp other kids.

Threatening had worked for her. Nobody teased Jenny. **But she didn't have any friends.**

"Well, I have to go," Jenny said. "My dad's taking me bowling. I just love smashing pins." She slammed her fist against her hand.

"See you tomorrow, Jenny," Becca said. She smiled at Jenny.

"At lunch," Monica added. "I mean, **if you want to sit with us**, that is."

Jenny looked surprised. I knew that Monica had stopped sitting with her in second grade after Jenny flattened the **chocolate cake.**

Most days, Jenny ended up sitting by herself at lunch. She didn't seem to mind, but I know **I'd feel lonely** if I ate by myself every day. After all, lunch was the best part of the middle school day!

I thought about it. It wouldn't be so bad if Jenny sat with us at lunch.

"Do you want to get back at Anna and Carly?" Jenny asked.

"Maybe," Monica said.

"I know **the best revenge**," Becca said. "Doing a project that gets an A."

"But we don't have a fantastic idea," Monica said.

"**Optical illusions**," Jenny suggested. "You can find all kinds of help online."

Becca and Monica looked at each other. They both seemed surprised.

Becca said, "That's a great idea."

"**Duh,**" Jenny said. Then she left.

CHAPTER 8

PAYBACK

The next day, Becca and Monica gave their report first.

"Our new science project is **a feast for the eyes**," Monica said.

"You'll be totally amazed!" Becca exclaimed.

"I'll be totally **freaked out** if my eyes start eating feasts," Tommy joked.

Monica waited until the class stopped laughing. Then she continued, "First we'll show some **unbelievable** optical illusions."

"Then we'll solve the mystery," Becca added.

"What mystery?" Adam asked.

Tommy softly hummed *creepy movie music.*

Becca lowered her voice dramatically and asked, "Why do certain patterns fool the eye?"

"Why do they?" Brad Turino asked.

Peter started to raise his hand, but he stopped. He was the class brain, so I knew he knew the answer, but he didn't want to RUIN Monica and Becca's fun.

Monica grinned. "Tune in next Monday to find out," she said.

"**Excellent** idea, girls!" Mr. Monroe said. "Your project is approved."

I gave my friends two **thumbs-up**.

Becca gave me an **OK sign**.

Jenny gave Monica a **high five**.

"What do you have, Anna?" Mr. Monroe asked.

Anna stood up. "Carly and I are going to study how plants react to different conditions."

Mr. Monroe frowned. "That's the same project you had yesterday."

"Yes, but now we're the ONLY team doing it," Anna explained. "Monica and Becca already have a new project."

"I told both teams to come in with new projects," the teacher said. "Monica and Becca did the extra work. I'm sorry, Anna, but it's not fair to let you do the plant project."

NOTE #1: Anna thinks she's always right. She also thinks everyone will give her what she wants. They mostly do.

NOTE #2: Mr. Monroe is one of the people who doesn't follow Anna's rules.

Anna argued, "Monica and Becca said it was okay."

"It's not okay with **me**," Mr. Monroe said.

Anna narrowed her eyes. "But —" she started.

Mr. Monroe stopped her. "Please have a new project and summary tomorrow," he told her.

After class, Becca, Monica, and I huddled in the hall.

"That was so AWESOME!" Monica said. She sounded delighted. "I couldn't believe it. Did you see the look on Anna's face?"

"She was **totally stunned**," I said. "Anna couldn't believe that Mr. Monroe said no. It was amazing! I love it when Anna gets what she deserves."

"I'm so glad she didn't get away with pushing us around," Becca said.

Jenny walked over. "I should have STOMPED Anna in the first grade when I wanted to," she said, rolling her eyes.

"What did Anna do to you?" Becca asked.

Jenny hesitated. Then she shrugged and told us, "Somebody gave me some cookies, and then Anna *embarrassed* me."

"How?" I asked.

"She said, 'You eat too many cookies, Jenny! Maybe that's why you're too tall. You eat too much and grow too fast,'" Jenny told us. Her face got all scrunched up. It was the same face Nick made when he was mad.

It was seven years later, and **Jenny was still mad at Anna.**

"I hate being embarrassed," Jenny said.

Monica, Becca, and I nodded. We knew exactly how Jenny felt. Anna had embarrassed 𝔼𝕍𝔼ℝ𝕐𝕆ℕ𝔼 in school.

After Jenny left, my friends and I headed to fourth period history.

"Now we know why Jenny acts so tough," I said.

"And why she got mad at me in second grade," Monica added.

"The time when you opened her milk carton?" Becca asked.

Monica nodded. "I was just trying to help. But **Jenny was insulted**," she said.

I said, "Ronnie Carver called Jenny names, and Anna was nasty. No wonder she wanted to stomp them." Then I realized something.

Name calling, teasing, and making rude remarks were bullying too. When Jenny was five, she decided not to take it.

She fought back.

That's why Jenny Pinski was the class bully. Not because she was **born mean**. Because people had teased her until she had to put a stop to it.

Of course, Jenny Pinski was still mean when someone made her mad. So I still had to be careful.

I hadn't done anything to make Jenny mad.

Yet.

CHAPTER 9

JENNY KNOWS BEST

Wednesday: Planet Properties

Our science projects were due on Monday. **We didn't have much time.**

Jenny and I sat together at lunch again. We compared research notes.

"I searched the Internet," Jenny said.

"I did too," I said. "I also used the library."

"Read this," Jenny said. She handed me her notes. "My rock life planet is PERFECT."

I took Jenny's papers. Then I handed her my notebook.

"What's this?" Jenny asked.

"My outline," I said. "Read it. **In case you missed something.**"

Jenny shrugged and started reading.

When she finished, she said, "Your outline is the same as my notes!"

Another good thing about Jenny:
Jenny Pinski is smart.

"Good!" I exclaimed. "This is a science project. Our facts should match. We both figured out the perfect planet for rock people."

The Properties of Weird World:

A Planet Where Rocks Rule

1. Very close to sun

2. 900 degrees Fahrenheit (like Venus)

3. Liquid iron oceans

4. Gaseous sulfur/oxygen atmosphere

5. Crystal life forms

    A. Quartz (many colors)

    B. Copper (green)

    C. Glass or fiberglass (sand, many colors)

6. Oxidation of iron (rock food) = energy

Jenny gave my outline back. "I'm glad we agree," she said. "I already started the model."

I went to Jenny's house on the way home from school. She wanted me to see her progress.

"I only have one diorama done," Jenny said. She held up a shoebox with a rock planet scene inside. "It's a **crystal forest** with rock animals. What do you think?"

I gasped. Then I cleared my throat to cover it.

Jenny's little rock animals were cute. They had  heads, blue rhinestone eyes, and stubby little legs. But the crystal trees were limp paper cutouts. **They looked horrible.**

"What are those?" I asked, pointing to the yellow lines Jenny had painted on the rocks.

"Crystal pathways," Jenny said. "They're inside the rock creatures, like veins. **Rock life uses electricity instead of blood.**"

I had done a lot of research. I knew that crystals conducted electricity, so Jenny's idea made sense. In fact, it might help us get an A. But **that's not why I was upset.**

I hated Jenny's paper trees. They looked horrible.

I had to say something.

"We should make some simple crystals," I said. "Epsom salt and borax crystals would make great trees and plants."

"I already have trees," Jenny said, frowning.

ⓄⓄⓅⓈ! Jenny hated being criticized.

So I told her the diorama looked great.

Friday: Rejected Report

Jenny came to my house on Friday. My report was almost done. I sat on the sofa while she read the first draft.

Jenny didn't smile or nod or make a face. **I couldn't tell what she thought.** I tapped my foot and nibbled my knuckle until she finished.

"What do you think?" I asked.

Jenny stood up. She dropped my notebook on the coffee table. Then she said, "It's 𝔹𝕆ℝ𝕀ℕ𝔾."

Saturday: Weird Words

Jenny called my house on Saturday morning. She said that the planet model was done, and she wanted me to see it.

I said I would, but I hung up and asked myself: *Why bother, Claudia?*

If I didn't like the model, **Jenny would get mad.** I was pretty sure she wouldn't stomp me. But I was positive she wouldn't change the model. Not even if I had a better idea.

I went to see it anyway . . .

. . . and I was **jumping—for—joy thrilled!** Jenny's model of Weird World was fantastic.

"It's gorgeous!" I exclaimed.

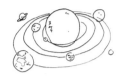

"**I know,**" Jenny said.

The gray planet had red oceans and wisps of yellow cotton clouds. There were three continents with little ridges for mountains.

"The oceans are red because iron rusts," Jenny explained.

I knew that. It was in my report. Our planet had an oxygen and sulfur atmosphere.

Oxygen breaks down iron (oxidation) = rust = red oceans

"Sulfur is yellow," Jenny explained. "That's why the clouds are yellow."

"All this information should be on a chart," I said.

"I'll do the chart later," Jenny said. "You have to write your report again."

"I already rewrote it last night," I said. "I worked on it for a long time. I'm sure it's **way more interesting** now."

"But you didn't use my notes," Jenny said. She handed me some papers. "My ideas will make our report **super exciting**."

I was *too chicken* to argue. I read Jenny's notes as I walked home. I felt sick when I reached my front porch.

Jenny wanted to use her idea about space explorers touring an alien planet again. Except this time, **a rock monster** squashed their rocket ship.

Jenny wanted our report to be **a science fiction adventure.**

I knew that Mr. Monroe wanted a scientific report. He wouldn't give us a good grade for turning in a story.

I had two choices. They were both bad.

I could settle for a B, maybe even a C. Or I could stand up to Jenny and write the report my way.

CHAPTER 10

A BETTER WAY

I did **not** rewrite my report. Instead, I spent all day making simple crystals.

The crystals needed time to form. And I needed advice. It was a **kid problem**, so I couldn't ask my parents. I asked my older brother.

Jimmy was in his bedroom. I knew he was playing a computer game because I could hear explosions through the closed door.

How To Annoy Your Older Brother

1. Don't knock. He'll lock the door and tell you to go away.

2. Barge in. He can't kick you out. Your mom will get mad.

3. If he won't talk to you, wait.

4. If he keeps ignoring you, play with his stuff.

I barged in without knocking. "I have to ask you something," I told him.

"I'm busy," Jimmy said.

"It's really IMPORTANT," I insisted.

"Don't care," Jimmy said. His fingers flew over his keyboard. He didn't stop watching his screen.

There was a comic book on Jimmy's bed. I picked it up. "Is this the new **Micro—Marauders**?" I asked innocently.

Jimmy paused his game and turned around. "What do you want?"

I carefully put the comic book back on the bed. Jimmy would get cranky if the corners got bent. "Did a **bully** ever come after you?" I asked.

Jimmy nodded. "**A big kid** picked on me when I was nine," he told me.

"What did he do?" I asked.

I wanted to hear details. I thought maybe the details of Jimmy's story would help me **solve my problem.**

"He said he'd punch me if I didn't do what he wanted," Jimmy said. "I gave him my lunch money for a month."

"What happened after a month?" I asked.

"I went to Dad for advice," Jimmy explained. "He asked me, '*What's the worst that can happen?*' And I said, 'John Jones will **punch my lights out**.'"

I giggled.

Jimmy went on, "Then Dad said, 'You've got to stand up for yourself. Getting punched won't be **as bad** as you think.'"

I gasped. "**Our dad** said that?" I asked. I was shocked.

"Yep," Jimmy said. "The next day I told John Jones he couldn't have my money. And he punched me in the jaw."

I winced. "Did it 𝐻𝑈𝑅𝑇?" I asked.

"Not as much as I thought it would," Jimmy said. He grinned. "And after that, John Jones left me alone."

I didn't feel better when I left Jimmy's room. But I knew what to do.

I called Jenny and asked her to come over.

"Are you done with the new report?" Jenny asked when she walked in.

I couldn't put off the **dreadful deed**. I had to do what I thought was right even if Jenny got mad. Jimmy had taken a punch in the jaw. I could take a little 𝕊𝕋𝕆𝕄ℙ𝕀ℕ𝔾.

I took a deep breath. "I didn't write a new report," I told her.

"Why not?" Jenny asked, frowning. "Didn't you like my notes?"

"Mr. Monroe wants a report that explains our project facts," I said. "Your story would make a great movie, but I don't think it will get an A from our science teacher."

Jenny scrunched up her face.

This time I had three choices.

They were all bad.

1. Fight back.

2. Take it.

3. Run away.

I braced myself. I waited to see what Jenny would do.

Jenny exhaled. "You're right, Claudia. Mr. Monroe won't like an EXCITING, action-packed story," she said.

I was shocked! I had stood up to Jenny Pinski, and **I was still standing**!

She wasn't even a little bit mad. But she looked pretty disappointed.

"And that's too bad," Jenny said. She sighed. "I really wanted our project to be super special."

"It will be!" I exclaimed. "We'll use your story ideas for the cards explaining the dioramas. Mr. Monroe won't care if our display looks like an **exciting adventure**."

Jenny smiled. "That's a great idea, Claudia!" she said.

"I've got more ideas," I said. "If you want to hear them."

Jenny frowned again. "Go on," she said slowly.

I kept talking. "I have some of my mom's crystal pieces." Jenny looked confused. I kept talking. "They make **bell sounds** when you tap them. Like rock people language," I explained.

"ᏟᎤᎤᏞ!" Jenny exclaimed. "Rock people have to talk to each other. That's brilliant."

"And I made some simple crystals to show you," I added. "Follow me." I took Jenny into the kitchen.

The Epsom salt sheet crystals were spidery. They looked like delicate, alien shrubs. I had grown the borax crystals on pipe cleaners shaped like trees.

"These are **awesome**," Jenny said. "I should have listened to you before."

"Better now than never," I joked. "These crystals are **easy to make**. We'll have plenty for the dioramas. And we can use them as examples of inorganic stuff that grows!"

"Three types of crystals will definitely get us an A," Jenny said.

"You know what's better than one head?" I asked.

"Two project partners!"

Jenny gave me a high five.

CHAPTER 11

P.S.

Jenny didn't want to hang out with me after the project was done. She liked **bowling, karate, and BMX racing.** Compared to that, Becca, Monica, and I were 𝕭𝕺𝕽𝕴𝕹𝕲.

Anna and Carly studied how weather conditions affect hair. They had their friends model limp, frizzy, and sun-bleached hair. The other girls weren't happy, but the presentation was **hilarious.**

Becca and Monica's Optical Illusion Mystery was a **huge hit**. They explained that eyes and minds evolved to recognize things that help us survive and relate to the world. When we look at a pattern that doesn't exist in nature, we see things that aren't correct.

Nick still had a Caroline problem. She stopped calling him pea-brain and **kissed him!** Caroline liked Nick, which was a zillion times worse for a seven-year-old boy than being pushed in a puddle.

Oh, and **Jenny and I got an A** for our project. Mr. Monroe thought our scientific paper was great, and everyone loved the rock-monster-squashes-a-rocket diorama.

I realized that sometimes, **Jenny** scrunched up her face and looked mad because she was thinking. She also scrunched up her face and looked mad when she was mad. So I still watched what I said and did. **Better safe than stomped!**

About the Author

Diana G. Gallagher lives in Florida with her husband and five dogs, four cats, and a cranky parrot. Her hobbies are gardening, garage sales, and grandchildren. She has been an English equitation instructor, a professional folk musician, and an artist. However, she had aspirations to be a professional writer at the age of twelve. She has written dozens of books for kids and young adults.

About the Illustrator

Brann Garvey lives in Minneapolis, Minnesota with his wife, Keegan, their dog, Lola, and their very fat cat, Iggy. Brann graduated from Iowa State University with a bachelor of fine arts degree. He later attended the Minneapolis College of Art and Design, where he studied illustration. In his free time, Brann enjoys being with his family and friends. He brings his sketchbook everywhere he goes.

Glossary

announced (uh-NOUNSSD)—said publicly

approve (uh-PROOV)—to officially accept an idea

contraption (kuhn-TRAP-shuhn)—a strange or odd device or machine

detector (di-TEK-tur)—a machine that reveals the presence of something

diorama (dye-oh-RAH-muh)—a three-dimensional model representing a scene

exceptions (ek-SEP-shuhnz)—something that is not included in a general rule or statement

inorganic (in-or-GAN-ik)—not coming from living things

optical illusion (OP-tuh-kuhl i-LOO-zhuhn)—something that tricks the eyes into seeing something that isn't there

oral (OR-uhl)—spoken

reigned (RAYND)—ruled as king or queen

sarcastic (sar-KASS-tik)—if you are sarcastic, you use bitter or joking words that make fun of something

silicon (SIL-uh-kuhn)—a chemical element found in sand and rocks

summary (SUHM-ur-ee)—a short statement that gives the main ideas of something

threaten (THRET-uhn)—frighten or put in danger

1. Why doesn't Claudia want to work with Jenny? How do you think she will feel if she is paired up with Jenny on a future project? Talk about your answers.

2. When Anna and Carly have the same idea for a project as Becca and Monica, their teacher asks them to come up with new project ideas. Do you think that was fair? Why or why not?

3. Why is Jenny Pinski a bully?

Writing Prompts

1. Have you ever had to deal with a bully? Write about your experience.

2. Create your own Weird World. Then draw a picture of it, or build a diorama. What kinds of plants or animals live on your Weird World?

3. In this book, Claudia realizes that Jenny isn't as mean as she thought. Write about a time when you discovered that someone was different from what you expected. What did you think about the person before? What happened? What do you think about the person now?

MORE FUN with Claudia!

THE COMPLICATED LIFE OF

Claudia
Cristina
Cortez

BY DIANA G. GALLAGHER

HIRED OR FIRED?

Claudia Cristina Cortez

Just like every other thirteen-year-old girl, Claudia Cristina Cortez has a complicated life. Whether she's studying for the big Quiz Show, babysitting her neighbor, Nick, avoiding mean Jenny Pinski, planning the seventh-grade dance, or trying desperately to pass the swimming test at camp, Claudia goes through her complicated life with confidence, cleverness, and a serious dash of cool.

MORE fun

DAVID MORTIMORE BAXTER

David is a great kid, but he has one big problem — he can't stop talking. These wildly humorous stories, told by David himself, will show readers just how much trouble a boy and his mouth can get into, whether he's going on a class trip, trying to find a missing neighbor, running a detective agency, or getting lost in the wild. David is amiable, engaging, cool, and smart enough to realize that growing up is the biggest adventure of all.

with David!